American Folktales for the primary grades, full of action and humor, are about America's best known and most loved folklore characters. Told in true tall-tale manner, each story has a simple plot and colorful illustrations. These delightful books, sure to appeal to beginning readers everywhere, are ideal for individualized or independent reading in the classroom or library.

Dan McCann
and His Fast
Sooner Hound

by Irwin Shapiro

illustrated by Mimi Korach

GARRARD PUBLISHING COMPANY
CHAMPAIGN, ILLINOIS

Dan McCann and His Fast Sooner Hound

Over the hills and across the valley went the train. The engine chugged. The whistle blew. The bell rang. The wheels went clickety-clack on the tracks.

And running beside the train was Dan McCann's fast Sooner hound.

The Sooner was a big dog. He was white with black and brown spots. He had long, thin legs. He had a long tail with a kink in the middle. He had big, floppy ears, one black and one brown. And he was grinning a big, wide grin.

Rounding a bend, the Sooner passed the train. When the train pulled into the station, there was the Sooner. He was sitting on the platform, waiting for Dan.

The train stopped, and Dan hopped down from the cab of the engine. In his hand he carried his special long-handled shovel. Dan was the fireman on the train. His job was to shovel coal into the furnace of the engine. The furnace heated water, the water turned into steam, and the steam made the engine go.

Dan patted the Sooner on the head. A crowd gathered around them, looking at the Sooner. A little old man walked up on the platform. He pointed at the Sooner with his cane.

"Jumping jellybeans!" the little old man said. "I never saw a critter like that. What is it?"

"A fast Sooner hound," said Dan. "He'd sooner run than eat.

And he'd sooner eat than sleep.
But he'd sooner run than anything.
That's why he's called a Sooner."

"Heh!" said the little old man.
"A Sooner, is he? Fast, is he? He
doesn't look so fast to me."

The Sooner stopped grinning. Jumping over the crowd, he began running around the station.

Whooooooooooooooooosh!

He ran so fast he couldn't be seen. He raised a wind like a small cyclone. The wind blew off people's hats and scattered papers.

It almost blew the people off the platform.

"Help!" everyone cried. "Help! Look out! Hold on!"

A tall man with a long moustache came rushing out of the station. He was the roadmaster who ran the railroad.

"What's going on here?" he
asked. "What's happening?"

But before Dan could answer,
whoomp, the Sooner ran into the
roadmaster and knocked him to
the ground. Dan helped him to
his feet and dusted him off.

"Sorry, roadmaster," he said.

"The Sooner didn't mean to knock you over. He was just trying to show how fast he can run."

"That Sooner dog!" yelled the roadmaster. He was so angry his moustache wiggled up and down. "The Sooner! I might have known. How many times have I told you? This is no place for a dog. You'll have to get rid of him!"

"I couldn't do that," said Dan. "I raised him from a pup. He goes where I go, and I go where he goes."

"Then I'll have to get rid of *you*," shouted the roadmaster.

"You can't fire me!" said Dan.

"Why not?" the roadmaster shouted.

"Because I quit!" said Dan.

Dan picked up his special long-handled shovel, and he went home. The Sooner went with him. The Sooner's tail drooped, and his head hung low.

Dan smiled.

"It's all right, Sooner," he said. "It wasn't your fault. Besides, I'll get another job. I hear the C.B.&Q. railroad in Philadelphia needs firemen."

Dan packed his clothes in a suitcase. Then, with his suitcase in one hand and his special long-handled shovel in the other, he set out for Philadelphia. At the C.B.&Q. station, he went into the roadmaster's office. The Sooner waited outside.

This roadmaster had a bald head and puffed on a big cigar. He looked up from his desk. Then he said, "I see by your shovel that you are a fireman."

"Right," said Dan. "And my name is Dan McCann."

"And you're looking for a job," the roadmaster said.

"Right again," said Dan.

"I could use a good fireman," the roadmaster said. "And you look good to me. You're hired."

Before Dan could say thank
you, the door burst open.
Whooooooooooooooosh!
Something that was like a
small cyclone came tearing into the
room. Papers from the desk flew
around. The roadmaster was so
scared he hid behind his desk.

"Don't be scared, roadmaster," said Dan. "It's just my fast Sooner hound. He wouldn't hurt a fly."

The roadmaster peeped over the top of the desk. Sure enough, standing near Dan was the Sooner.

The roadmaster rubbed his bald head.

"You'll have to find some place to leave him," he said.

"Can't be done," said Dan. "He'd howl and yowl and cry his eyes out. The Sooner goes where I go, and I go where he goes."

"Sorry," said the roadmaster. "But he can't ride with you on the train. It's against the rules."

"The Sooner doesn't ride," Dan said. "He just runs along beside the train."

"You mean to say he keeps up with the train?" the roadmaster asked.

"Oh, no," Dan answered. "Most of the time he runs ahead of it. He gets to the station before I do and he waits for me."

The roadmaster laughed so hard he almost choked on his cigar.

"Dan McCann," he said, "you're a joker. I'll tell you what. I'll put you on train number 23 to Allentown and back. It's not very fast, but it's faster than any dog.

If the Sooner gets to the station here before you do, I'll buy you the best dinner at the Blue Goose Restaurant."

"Suits me," said Dan. "But I warn you, the Sooner is the fastest thing on four legs."

The next morning, Dan put on his overalls and his trainman's cap.

He picked up his special long-handled shovel and went to the railroad yard. The Sooner went with him.

Dan climbed into the cab of the engine and started to shovel coal. When the train pulled out, the Sooner trotted beside it.

The Sooner didn't really run.

He didn't have to. The train was too slow.

To make it more interesting, he ran in big circles around the train. Or he ran off into the fields to sniff the flowers. Of course, he got to the station long before the train.

The roadmaster waited on the platform. When he saw the Sooner, he almost swallowed his cigar.

"I see it," he said. "I see it, but I don't believe it. No dog can run faster than a train."

Ten minutes later the train rolled in. The roadmaster took Dan to the Blue Goose for dinner.

Dan ordered chicken and potatoes and green peas and apple pie with ice cream on top. The Sooner had a nice bone.

The roadmaster didn't eat a thing. But he wasn't ready to give up yet.

"Dan," he said, "I'm putting you on train number 34. It goes to Harrisburg and back. Every time the Sooner gets to the station first, I'll buy you a dinner."

"Suits me," said Dan.

The next day Dan started shoveling coal on train number 34. It was faster than the other train, and the Sooner had to run a little. All the same, he was at the station before Dan.

"It's just a trick!" yelled the roadmaster. "That Dan McCann is tricking me with the Sooner hound! And by thunder, I'll find out how!"

Each day the roadmaster went to the station. Each day he hid behind a baggage truck and watched. Each day he saw the Sooner come running in before the train. And each day he bought Dan a dinner.

Even worse, the Sooner was making the railroad look bad. One day the roadmaster heard the passengers talking.

"Is this any way to run a railroad?" shrieked a lady with a long feather on her hat.

The roadmaster jumped out from behind the baggage truck.

"Excuse me, ma'am," he said. "I'm the roadmaster of this railroad. What is the trouble?"

"Trouble?" said a man with bushy eyebrows. "I'll tell you what's the trouble. You've got the slowest trains on earth, that's what!"

"You're wrong, sir. Our trains are always on time," the road-master said.

"How can they be on time?" shouted the lady with the feather on her hat. "We saw that dog running ahead of the train. If a train can't keep up with a dog, it must be mighty slow!"

"We might as well walk," said the man with the bushy eyebrows. "I'll never ride on this train again!"

The roadmaster was so angry he could have bitten a rail in two. He rushed over to the Sooner, who was sitting on the platform.

"You slab-sided mutt!" he yelled. "You're ruining the railroad! You're ruining me!"

The Sooner wagged his tail and grinned.

"Bah!" said the roadmaster.

He ran into his office and slammed the door.

"Oh, that Sooner, that Sooner!" he wailed. "What am I going to do? I've got to stop him."

The roadmaster was a proud man. He didn't like anybody getting the best of him, let alone a dog. And he was a stubborn man. He didn't like to give up anything he started.

"I can't let a dog make a fool out of me," he said. "I've got to beat the Sooner. But how? How?"

He walked up and down. He rubbed his bald head. He puffed on his cigar until the room was filled with smoke.

"I've got it!" he said, banging his fist on the desk. "I'll fix that Sooner, once and for all. I'll send Dan out on the Cannonball Express!

It's the fastest thing on wheels. It will leave the Sooner miles behind. And just to make sure, I'll be the engineer myself!"

The roadmaster ordered a clear track all the way to Chicago for the Cannonball.

The trainmen told their friends, "The Cannonball is going to race the Sooner!"

The trainmen's friends told their friends. Everybody talked about it. On the day of the race, people lined the tracks for miles.

The roadmaster climbed up into the cab with Dan. They were both wearing overalls and trainmen's caps. Dan was carrying his special long-handled shovel.

"No tricks, Dan," said the roadmaster. "No holding back. Just keep shoveling coal. Pour it on. Are you ready?"

"I'm ready," said Dan.

The roadmaster stuck his head out the window.

"Ready?" he said to the Sooner.

"Yipe!" barked the Sooner, grinning and wagging his tail.

"Then *go!*" said the roadmaster.

The Cannonball chugged and puffed as it started down the tracks. The roadmaster blew a blast on the whistle. He rang the

bell. The engine roared, louder than thunder.

"Faster!" the roadmaster shouted. "More coal, Dan! Pour it on!"

And Dan poured it on. He shoveled so hard and so fast that sparks flew from his special long-handled shovel. The train went streaking along, with the Sooner running beside it.

They went so fast that a man couldn't watch them by himself. It took three men to do it.

The first man would say, "Here they come!"

The second man would say, "Here they are!"

Then the third man would say, "There they go!"

To tell the truth, all anybody could see was smoke and steam rushing along the tracks. Nobody could tell whether or not the Sooner was keeping up with the Cannonball.

When the Cannonball rolled into the station at Chicago, the crowd sent up a cheer.

Dan and the roadmaster jumped down from the engine.

"Where's the Sooner?" Dan asked.

"He's nowhere in sight," the crowd answered.

"Did you hear that?" yelled the roadmaster. "He's nowhere in sight. I beat the Sooner! I beat him at last!"

He laughed. He waved his arms. He jumped up and down.

He threw his cap into the air.
And he lit a big cigar.

Dan shook his head slowly.

"I can't believe it," he said.
"I can't believe it. The Sooner's
never been beaten before."

Then a man in a white shirt came running out of the station. He pushed through the crowd.

"A message just came in by telegraph," he said. "The Sooner was seen passing the station in Rockford!"

"By cracky!" shouted Dan. "The Sooner went by here so fast nobody could see him! He was way ahead of the train!"

In a minute the man in the white shirt was back.

"Here's another message," he said. "The Sooner just passed the station in Cedar Rapids. He was heading west and still running!"

"You know what?" said Dan. "The Sooner is out to break all records. He won't stop till he gets to San Francisco!"

"Come on," yelled the road-master, pulling Dan toward the train.

"Where are we going?" asked Dan.

"To San Francisco," said the roadmaster. "This race isn't over yet. No dog is going to get the best of me. If I don't beat the Sooner, I'll quit the railroad!"

"And if the Sooner doesn't beat you, *I'll* quit," said Dan. "And the Sooner will never run against a train again!"

"Then let's go," the roadmaster said. "He's got a head start, and I've got to catch up."

Quickly they climbed up into the cab of the engine. The roadmaster blew the whistle and rang the bell. Dan shoveled coal.

The engine chugged. Away went the Cannonball down the tracks, heading west.

On and on streaked the Cannonball, by day and by night, over mountains and across plains. Past cities and towns, past forests and farms, it went. And still there was no sign of the Sooner.

"We must have passed him in the night," said the roadmaster.

"We didn't," said Dan.

"We did," said the roadmaster.

"Didn't!" said Dan.

"Did!" said the roadmaster.

Then, just as they were getting near the station at San Francisco,

they saw the Sooner. He was
running by the tracks.

"There he is," the roadmaster
shouted. "We're catching up! We've
caught up! We're even! More coal,
Dan! Full steam ahead! I'll beat
the Sooner yet!"

The Cannonball, still chugging
and puffing, pulled into the station.
So did the Sooner. The Cannonball
stopped. The Sooner stopped.

A great shout went up from
the crowd of people at the station.

"They're here," they cried. "The

Cannonball is here. The Sooner is here. But who won?"

Dan and the roadmaster jumped down to the tracks. They looked at the Cannonball, and they looked at the Sooner. The Sooner's nose was exactly even with the front end of the engine.

"It's a tie!" shouted the crowd.

"They're right," said Dan and the roadmaster sadly.

"I didn't beat the Sooner," said the roadmaster, rubbing his bald head.

"The Sooner didn't beat the Cannonball," said Dan, sighing.

The Sooner's tail drooped. He hung his head, and tears came into his eyes.

Then out of the crowd came the mayor of San Francisco. He was wearing a top hat and a long-tailed coat.

The mayor shook the roadmaster's hand. He shook Dan's hand. He patted the Sooner on the head. Everyone in the crowd cheered. They cheered Dan and the roadmaster, the Cannonball and the Sooner.

"Why are they cheering?" asked the roadmaster. "The Cannonball didn't beat the Sooner. I'm going to quit the railroad."

"And the Sooner didn't beat the Cannonball," said Dan. "I'm going to quit too."

"Quit?" said the mayor. "Don't be silly. The Cannonball and the Sooner broke all records. You have the fastest train and the fastest dog in the world. The whole country will be talking about you.

Everybody will want to ride on your trains and see the Sooner."

"By cracky, he's right!" said the roadmaster to Dan.

He jabbed Dan in the ribs. Dan pounded him on the back.

They whooped. They hollered. The Sooner grinned and wagged his tail. He stood up on his hind legs and danced a little jig with Dan and the roadmaster.

After that, Dan and the

roadmaster and the Sooner went back to the C.B.&Q. railroad. Just as the mayor said, the whole country was talking about them. Crowds came to ride the trains and see the Sooner.

Ever since that time, dogs have been running along beside railroad tracks. But they never will run as fast as the trains. Not until another dog comes along like Dan McCann's fast Sooner hound.